To Primrose, who makes the hugging rules, and Wisteria, who ignores them.

Pipweasel

My Hugging Rules, Copyright © 2019 by David Kirk.
All rights reserved.
For information, contact Pipweasel, PO Box 25, King Ferry, NY 13081.
The illustrations in this book are charcoal drawings on paper with digital colorization.

Publisher's Cataloging-in-Publication Data
Names: Kirk, David, 1955-, author.
Title: My hugging rules / David Kirk.
Description: King Ferry, NY: Pipweasel, LLC: 2019.
Summary: A cat has a set of rules for how her friends can hug her, but when she needs a hug,
she discovers that her very particular rules need to be changed.
Identifiers: ISBN 978-1-7326861-0-6
Subjects: LCSH: Cats--Juvenile fiction. | Hugging--Juvenile fiction. | Rules--Juvenile fiction.
| Behavior--Juvenile fiction. | Humorous stories--Juvenile fiction.
| CYAC: Cats. | Hugging. | Rules. | Humorous stories. | Behavior.
| BISAC: JUVENILE FICTION / Animals / Cats |
Classification: LCC PZ8.3.K6554 My 2019 | DDC [E]--dc23

1 3 5 7 9 10 8 6 4 2
Printed in the USA. First Edition 2019

pipweasel.com

my Hugging RULES

DAVID KIRK

This handbook is your official guide to giving me a hug.

Study the following pages carefully before proceeding to actual hugging.

Hugs are to be given gently,

respectfully,

and without matting or otherwise ruffling my fur.

When I have reached my daily hug limit, you may choose to be put on a waiting list for the next available opening.

There shall be no head hugs,

no leg hugs,

and no tail hugs.

Cheek hugs are frowned upon.

Please do not hug me while looking ridiculous,

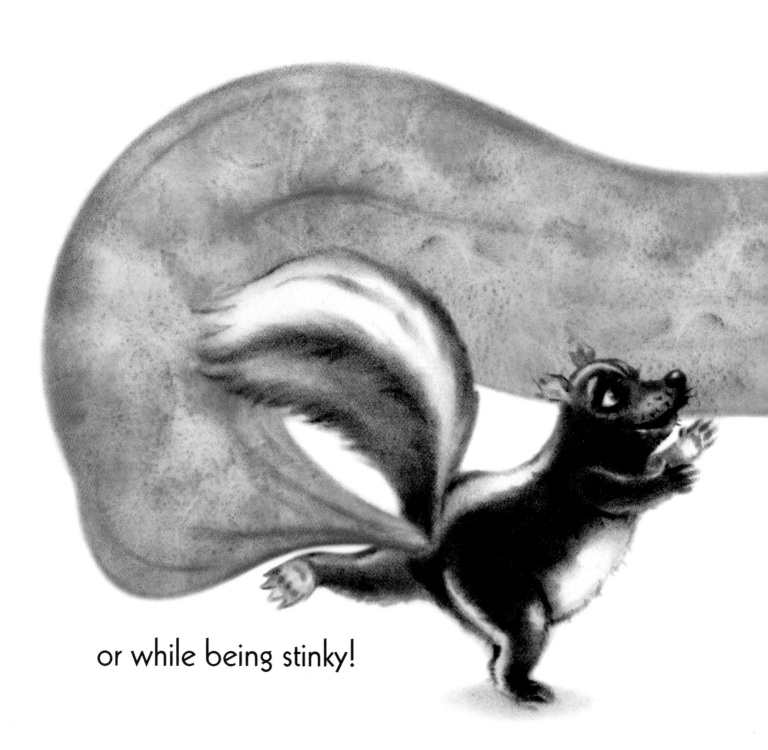

or while being stinky!

Do not hug me if your feet are dripping,
or if you are on the potty,

or if your nose is dripping,

or if I am on the potty!

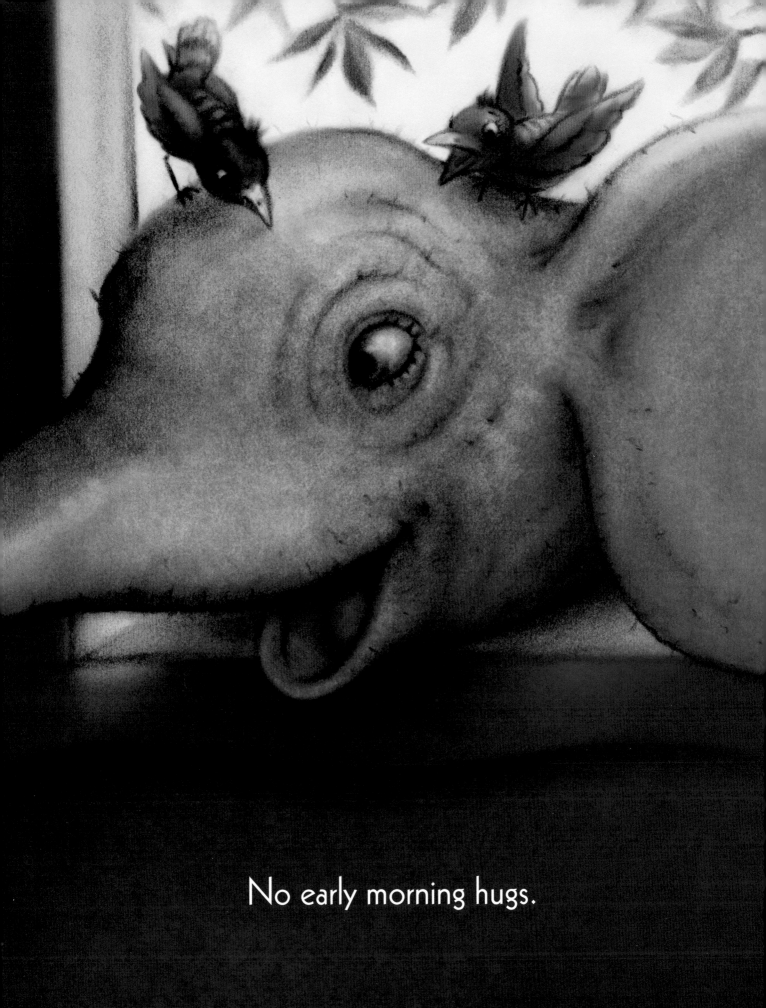

No early morning hugs.

No pinchy hugs.

No swishy, swoopy hugs.

I do not allow traveling hugs,

or hugs with a loady diaper,

or hugs with no diaper!

No scaly hugs, thank you,

Or prickly hugs.

Falling from above hugs are strictly prohibited,

and I do not permit hugs with
three or more arms.

Bear hugs are not permitted,
especially if you are a bear.

And please,
no
much,
much
too
tight
hugs.

Anybody need a hug?

Please?

Time for new rules!

Ready?

Head hugs,
leg hugs,
tail hugs, OK!

Pinchy hugs,
gently please.

Ridiculous hugs
gladly accepted,

as well as stinky hugs.

Falling from above hugs, WHAHOO!

Swishy, swoopy
hugs, WHEEEE!

Just right hugs? Yes.

Early morning
hugs, good.
Late morning hugs,
even better.

Bear hugs are encouraged,
especially if you are a bear.

Potty hugs —
just a minute, please.

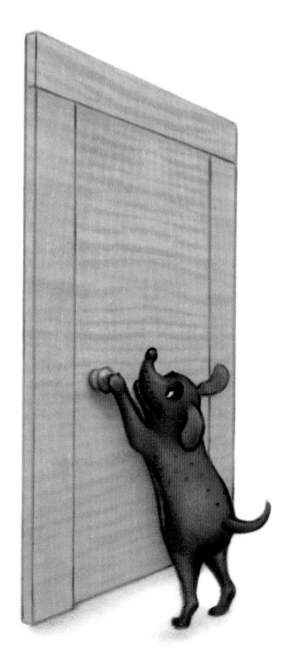

Cheek hugs bring a smile.

Drippy hugs —
OK, ready.

And loady diaper hugs,
well....

Ah, that's
loads better.

I welcome
prickly hugs,

scaly hugs,

and the more arms the merrier!

Now, who
needs a hug?

How about you?